Speechless

Library of Congress Control Number: 2015943909

ISBN: 978-1-63308-163-5 (paperback)
ISBN: 978-1-63308-164-2 (ebook)

Cover and Interior Design by R'tor John D. Maghuyop

CHALFANT ECKERT
PUBLISHING

1028 S Bishop Avenue, Dept. 178
Rolla, MO 65401

Printed in the United States of America

Speechless

HALEY NICOLE

CHALFANT ECKERT

PUBLISHING

TABLE OF CONTENTS

ACKNOWLEDGEMENT

Special thanks to special teachers who inspired me not only
to write, but helped me through the process:

Kim Farris
Claudette Gormley
Rebecca Proctor
Darlena Starner

I could not have done it without them and
I will be forever grateful.

CHAPTER 1

Me & My Bestie

When I was born, there were a lot of complications. My mother died and I couldn't speak. I said my first word at the age of four. Now, I am fifteen, and my name is Julia. I live with my brother, Danny because our father killed himself when I was ten. My brother is now eighteen, but he was only thirteen when our dad died. We live with our great grandfather, *Pa*, who has some memory problems. He is in the hospital, and he also has a lot of money.

My best friend is a boy named Sam. Danny and Sam are the only ones who understand my mumbles. I can say yes, no, and a couple of other one syllable words. Danny and I live in Pa's house which is across the street from where Sam lives. He has two older brothers. One is the same age as Danny, named Seth and the other is in college. His name is Shane. I call Sam's mom *Mama*

Renee. Sam's parents are divorced. I haven't seen Sam's dad in years and neither has he.

I have a Daschund named Topaz. When I mumble something, like paper, for example, she goes and gets me the paper. Topaz gets her name from her eyes. She has black and tan fur. In my opinion, Topaz is the best dog in the entire world. She is also around three years old. I got her when she was only about two months old. Topaz was a Christmas present one year from both Pa and Danny. She was the best Christmas present I had ever received.

I have long brunette hair that I love to braid. I do have bangs; they are swooped, short and tapered. Danny has the same hair. However, it is short. Both of us have gray eyes. Sam has green eyes that change to blue sometimes. His hair is a lovely, sandy-blonde color. His brothers don't share either of these traits. Sam gets them from his mother.

I hate it when people feel sorry for me. I mean, there are starving kids! Do something for them. Danny says to go with it which just makes me mad. I would like to help people instead. I can still make a difference and be different from most people. My voice may not be heard, but there are still many ideas floating around in my brain. They should be put to good use.

Pa gave Danny his car. It's an eight-year-old Chevy. I love to let the wind rush past me while riding in it. I also love to smile. I do have a horrible habit, I must chew gum! Danny's girlfriend, Heather, always buys me a pack. She is kind of an enabler of my gum chewing habit.

People ask me all the time if I can cry and scream. Yes, I can, but screaming just hurts my throat. However, it doesn't hurt to cry. I can also make noises in my mouth as long as I don't use my throat in any way. The throat is the only problem and the only thing that hurts so I cannot speak.

Sam and I are such good friends. I can tell him anything. However, we are nothing more than just friends. He plays football and so does Danny. I enjoy track, volleyball, and tennis. For tennis, the water girl shouts out what I can't. This girl is an eighth grader and also Heather's little sister, Paige. They both have straight, bright red hair and dark green eyes.

Sam and Paige are the only real friends I have. Most of the other kids make fun of me. However, it's not only the kids that make the jokes. Parents and teachers have also been caught making fun of me. I can only say this because I have personally heard them.

For some reason, when I got home, I remembered the song Sam had. He can play the guitar really well. Sam has written a total of five songs that I know of. It is one of his many hidden talents. However, Sam doesn't think so. At this moment in my thoughts, he came running over. I noticed that Sam was carrying a white envelope. He must have received it today in the mail because I hadn't seen it before, but that didn't mean much. Sam could have had it for a long time without me knowing it.

Sam didn't knock on the door, but then again, not many people did. It scared Danny and me when someone did knock on the door. He plopped down beside me on the couch. On the envelope was a blue stamp with a baby seal in the center. It looked expensive. The outside was written in computer type addressed to Sam. The envelope had already been opened so Sam had already seen what was inside. I pulled the letter out of the envelope, and it said:

Dear Sam,

> *I'm inviting you to my show. I want you to play some songs on your guitar for my viewers. I have heard all about your videos on the internet. I have watched a few, and I like them very much. If you decide to come, then you would be scheduled for the same day as Mr. Max Faulkner. As you can see, there are four tickets enclosed. Invite anyone you want. Hope to see you here.*

> *Sincerely,*
> *Kayte Burrow*

Sam was smiling at me. Grabbing a notebook, I wrote to him, "Wow! You get to meet Max Faulkner! He's my favorite actor."

Sam simply replied, "You silly gooney! You get to meet him too!" I lit up with excitement. "Danny's going to go with us too. I called Kayte Burrow, and her secretary, Vicky, said that Topaz could come too," Sam added.

I wrote him, "So happy. I love Max Faulkner!"

Sam turned his head in the other direction. The TV was on creating a distraction. At least is was for him.

I began to get lost in my own thoughts. In my opinion, Max Faulkner is a successful actor, singer, and model. He has shaggy hair that is as black as a night with a new moon. He also has blue eyes that sparkle like the sea or a twilight sky with a million stars to light it. I have a poster of Max Faulkner in my room. It has a black background so his tan skin shows up really well, and he is wearing a gray shirt. I have seen all of his movies. Max Faulkner is new to the Hollywood scene, but he has made quite a name for himself.

Sam got up and left my house. I noticed that he had left the envelope containing the letter. Running to the door, I clapped and stomped to get Sam's attention. Finally, he turned around and said, "Just keep it." He turned and started walking again. I stood in the doorway and watched Sam go into his house. Feeling a little stupid, I shut the door.

I went up to my room carrying Sam's envelope. He must have left it with me for some reason. I took the letter out and turned it over in my hands. On the back, there was a note written in odd handwriting.

Studying it more, it occurred to me that it was Sam's handwriting. It read:

Julia, you really should wear that shirt with red, gray, black and whites stripes on it. Not totally sure on that though. I'm going to wear a black shirt.

That solved my dilemma of what I was going to wear, but I wanted to impress my movie star crush. I should probably just be myself. Danny, Sam, and Mama Renee would be there with me. I had to remember that I was going as Sam's best friend and that this trip to the *Kayte Burrow Show* in Chicago was all about him. I was truly excited for I didn't get to travel very often.

CHAPTER 2

The Substitute

I hate it when there's a substitute. They always get mad when I don't answer. Today, our high school science teacher, Mr. Gibson, is going on a field trip to a farm with the freshmen class. Mr. Gibson said he would leave the substitute a note about me, but I brought one just in case. The sub was going to be Mr. Ray. I hadn't had him before.

Mr. Ray called everyone's names. On my name, I said "yes" instead of here. He gave me a dirty look. Perhaps he thought I was trying to be funny. I raised my hand and Mr. Ray said, "Come up here." So I got up out of my seat and went up to the desk. I handed Mr. Ray the note that said:

Julia has speech problems. She can only say yes and no. To answer your questions, she will write them down on a piece of paper. Thank you, Daniel Smith, older brother and guardian of Julia Smith.

"This is an excuse note?" Mr. Ray asked.

"Yes," I replied.

"I don't want this!" Mr. Ray shouted.

This got the attention of the whole class. However, most of them were already watching us. "Look at what you did. You got the class distracted." Mr. Ray threw the note at me and said, "Get back in your seat." I did so without saying anything.

Mr. Ray asked a question and called on me. I wrote the answer on a piece of paper and showed him. Somehow this must have offended him because he shouted, "That's it!" I looked at him with confusion. "Go to the office!" Mr. Ray screamed at me. At first, I thought he was joking. "Now!" Mr. Ray exclaimed.

When I crossed the hall and went into the office, the secretary, Mrs. Hampton stared at me. "What in the world are you in here for Miss Julia?" Mrs. Hampton asked me.

I wrote, "I don't know."

She kept looking at me and said, "I'll go find out." Mrs. Hampton left the office. When she returned, she told me to stay in the office with her until the hour was over.

During this time, Danny came in to make copies. "What'd she do?" he asked Mrs. Hampton.

"Absolutely nothing. The sub was mistaken," she said.

"That explains why she's just reading and not in trouble," Danny said.

"Yep, she's just going to stay in here till the hours up," Mrs. Hampton informed him

"Works for me," Danny said as he left.

I wasn't going to return to my class. This delighted me for I no longer had respect for Mr. Ray even though I had just met him.

I know that most people don't like me. They mock me all the time. Kids think I get special treatment, but I don't other than I don't answer many questions. Dirty looks here and there appear from my classmates and probably some others that I don't see or know about. This mocking and dislike started with Luke Jones. He didn't like Danny and he knew that if he made comments about me that Danny would get upset. Why Luke wanted the extra attention from Danny was a question I couldn't answer.

A funny feeling forced its way to my attention. Loud voices could be heard when I stepped out into the hall, which was unusual. One of the voices was definitely Danny. It was odd for him to be yelling during school. The other voice was more than likely Luke because Danny wouldn't be yelling at anyone else.

Heather stopped me in the hallway and said. "Hey Julia, would you like to have a girls' night out with Paige and me? We're going to go see the new Max Faulkner movie." Heather was trying to stall me from going to the senior hallway where the voices were coming from. Max Faulkner was my favorite actor, but I didn't care about what Heather was saying. I had to get to Danny and figure out what was going on. I ran past her and pushed past people in the hallway. Kids were circling to watch Danny and Luke fight. When some of the kids saw me, they opened a path to the center of the circle. Danny had poor Luke pinned in a corner.

"Stop!" I mumbled out in a scream. Danny stopped punching Luke, but still held him by his shirt collar. I started to cough painfully. Danny let Luke go when he saw something. I looked down and saw it too. My hands were splattered with red blood. I ran into the ladies' room.

Paige came with me and my coughing continued until I threw up. Paige held my hair while I was praying to the porcelain god.

Danny poked his head in the door. "Is anybody else in here?" he asked Paige. "Huh uh," she replied. I stopped praying and went to the sink to clean myself up.

When we all came out of the restroom, the principal was waiting for Danny. Danny got a three-day suspension, But Luke only got one day. Sam was waiting for me, and he walked me to my next class. I saw Heather later and guilt was splashed all across her face. I gave my stern eyes glare. Heather said, "I'm sorry." I nodded my head and went to my next class. There wasn't much else to do besides that. Heather was only doing what Danny had told her to do.

Sam's mom was having a birthday party and she invited me. I had absolutely no idea how old she was, but that didn't really matter. Danny, Heather, and Paige were coming with me to this party. Danny was invited and he won't go many places without Heather. Paige usually tags along with her sister.

I got Mama Renee a card and inside I taped a necklace on a silver chain. The pendant was purple with a heart shape, one of Mama Renee's favorite colors. I signed Danny's name to the card but didn't tell him. I didn't think he would care one way or another.

Seth is a really good cook, so he is making the meal for Mama Renee's birthday. I have been told that he is going to make fried chicken and baked potatoes. Sam said he wrote Mama Renee a song and he plans on playing it for everyone during the meal. Shane showed me a painting he made for Mama Renee.

Sam's grandparents came to Mama Renee's birthday lunch. I had only been around them a couple of times. Renee didn't have any siblings. However, I hadn't missed much. Sam's grandparents were sort of hateful. They left quickly after the meal, and after Mama Renee had opened her presents, Danny and his friends also left. But I stayed behind to help Mama Renee clean up. While we did dishes, Shane and Seth took Sam into the other room. I could hear everything they were saying, although I wasn't supposed to.

"Dude when are you going to make your move?" Shane asked.

"Yeah man. Julia's kind of pretty, I guess," Seth added.

"I don't know. She's way weird with the not being able to talk thing," Shane announced.

"Can too!" Sam shouted.

"I hope she can't hear us," Seth said.

"I don't care if she can," Shane said.

I dropped the dish I was drying. Tears ran down my cheeks.

"Julia?" Mama Renee urged. I turned around and ran from her. "Look at what you boys did!" Mama Renee exclaimed as I hurried out of their house. I really didn't want to stick around and hear the rest of the conversation.

I crashed on the couch when I got home. Danny was upstairs with Heather, and Paige was outside playing with my dog, which I needed to comfort me more than Paige needed a playmate.

The front door opened, and Sam ran inside. "Dude, are you okay?" he asked me. I didn't even look up at him. "Julia?" Sam asked as he collapsed next to me on the couch. I buried my face in the cushion and draped my legs over his as he stared at the television screen that wasn't turned on.

Sam moved me around so my hands were draped around his neck. My face was now just below Sam's shoulder on his chest. He played with my hair. Sam moved his chin to the top of my head. I just stayed where I was and cried and hoped I wasn't staining his shirt. When I finished crying, I reached for the notebook that was sitting on the coffee table in front of us. Sam whispered, "What's the matter, Julia?"

I wrote, "I heard the conversation between you and your brothers."

"I'm so sorry," Sam said.

"Do they really think that about me?" I asked.

"No, they say a lot of things they don't mean," he said.

"Do you think that?" I asked.

"No, of course not!" Sam exclaimed. He looked me in the eyes when I said that. "Do you want some strawberry soda?" Sam asked.

"Yes," I choked out.

He got up and went into my kitchen. Strawberry soda was my absolute favorite. When Sam came back in the living room and sat beside me again, our eyes locked. It was like in the movies. However, when we leaned in towards one another, Paige walked in. "Hey, Julia and Sam!" she exclaimed. I couldn't believe that Sam and I almost kissed.

Danny and Heather came noisily down the stairs. "I got to go," Sam said. He left my house without saying goodbye. Perhaps he was embarrassed by everyone being in the room. I know I sure was, but I didn't have an escape.

"Have you been crying?" Danny asked me. He stared at me with confusion.

"Yeah, sweetie?" Heather added.

I mouthed, "Fine."

"Okay then," Heather said. She didn't believe me, it wasn't her business, but I appreciated her concern. "Let's get out here."

"Not yet. Julia has to show me something in her room," Paige announced.

She must be lying because I didn't remember telling Paige anything like that.

"Oh! Okay," Heather answered with strange tone to her voice. She also stared at us like we were insane. Danny and Heather both sat down on the couch. They looked at each other before Danny turned on the television.

I headed up to my room, Paige at my heels with a big, goofy smile. I guessed that this was the first time she lied to her sister. I opened my door and led her inside. Paige plopped down on my bed and sat awkwardly. She was just about to speak when my phone vibrated. It was Sam. The text said, "Sorry. I'm blushing." I laughed.

"Oh my gosh, me too!" I replied to the text message.

"Is that Sam?" Paige asked. I just nodded. "Did you kiss him?" She asked.

Her question caught me off guard. "No," I said.

"But you almost did, right?" Paige asked.

"Yes," I replied.

"I won't tell anybody!" she exclaimed. "I think you guys would make a great couple," Paige added.

Heather yelled for Paige and our conversation was over. "We got to go now!" she shouted. "Bye," Paige said to me as she got up and left my bedroom. I just stood there in the middle of my room and stared at my cell phone.

CHAPTER 3

Preparing

S am's performance was coming up soon, so I started to pack. Tomorrow we would board a plane, land in Chicago, and go to our hotel. Danny, Mama Renee, Sam, and I would stay two nights. We decided to only take carry-on bags. I would have to share a hotel room with Danny. Each of us would have a queen size bed all to ourselves.

Seth was going to take us to the Spellman airport since Mama Renee didn't want to leave a car at the airport. For some reason, Seth didn't want to go to the show. Shane wanted to go, but he had a huge test in one of his college classes that he couldn't miss.

As I came down the stairs, Danny asked, "Are you ready for your haircut?" I thought this was the best time to get a haircut. My hair will look beautiful for the show. I would leave my hair down instead of putting it in a braid. I wanted to be different. At the salon, the lady cut my hair and styled it. I felt like a new woman.

The next day, we arrived at the airport. It wasn't crowded. Not many people flew out of this airport. On the plane, Danny sat by the window, I was in the middle, and Sam sat in the aisle seat. Mama Renee sat across the aisle from us. She was curled up with a book. "Do you want me to sit by you?" Sam asked his mom.

"Nope, I'm good. Sit with your friends," Mama Renee answered. "I got my book."

Danny turned to me and asked, "Are you feeling okay?" I nodded my head. "Are you excited?" he asked. I nodded again. "Me too," Danny added. "How 'bout you Sam?" he asked.

"I can't wait!" Sam shouted excitedly.

"Do we get to meet Max Faulkner?" Danny asked.

"Yep," Sam replied.

"Good because someone here really likes him," Danny said with a grin on his face.

"Are you having fun over there Julia?" Mama Renee sarcastically asked. I shrugged my shoulders.

During most of the plane ride, Danny and Sam made fun of me. Mama Renee got on to them as if they were five-year-olds. This made me laugh until I got in trouble too. Sam's mom was a mother for Danny and me too. However, we were pretty good kids for living on our own.

When Danny, Sam, Mama Renee, and I stepped out of the Chicago airport, we were able to hail a taxi right away. Danny sat up front. I was in between Sam and Mama Renee. All of a sudden, the taxicab came to a halt. To our right was the Hanson Inn and Suites. It was large like a skyscraper and marble looking. It was topped with a gray and black roof. I had never been to a hotel this nice before, and I was ready to enjoy the experience.

We walked inside a little bit confused. I could get lost in a place like this. The doors were huge and formed into silver arches. Two clerks sat at a desk just inside the hotel's entrance. "Did Kayte Burrow send you?" a short man asked us.

"Yes," Mama Renee replied.

"All four of you?" he asked.

"Yes sir," she said.

"There's a problem with the rooms. Miss Burrow told us to give you one room with two queen beds and another room with only one queen bed."

"It's okay. Julia and I can share," Danny said.

"Are you sure?" Mama Renee asked.

"Yes," I said.

Danny and Mama Renee were handed the hotel keys. We crossed the lobby and had an elevator to ourselves. Another couple boarded the other elevator. There was also the option to take the stairs, but I was fine with this. We got off on the third floor and no one was in the hallway. The rooms were across the hall from one another. We parted ways and entered our separate rooms.

"Which side of the bed do you want?" Danny asked. I pointed to the left side.

"Left?" he asked. I nodded my head. Danny turned on the TV and crashed on the bed. "Looks like your favorite show is on," he informed me. I sat down on the bed and watched the TV. It was actually a hilarious show. Danny was a fan too. Good thing too because I had only ever missed one episode, a real die-hard fan.

"Julia! Danny! Come here!" Sam shouted from the other room. I crossed the hall first, but Danny was right behind me. Thank goodness he grabbed the hotel key before shutting the door. My eyes nearly bugged out of my head because standing in front of me was Max Faulkner. He shook my hand and said, "Nice to meet you, Julia." I wanted to faint, but somehow I managed to hold myself together. "Hello Danny," Max Faulkner said as he shook my brother's hand.

Sam mouthed the words, "You're welcome," to me.

"Well I will see you tomorrow," Max Faulkner said just before he left. Danny and I returned to our room.

When we entered our room, my bag was moving. I was scared to open it, but I did it anyway. Inside was Topaz, my silly dog. She jumped right out. I got her some water, but she didn't drink any. "What a nice surprise!" Danny remarked. Topaz curled up on the shaggy carpet. It dawned on me that dogs don't travel in suitcases. Suitcases are thrown onto the airplane, routed with conveyer belts, and generally treated badly. The trip must have been hard on Topaz, and she would not be going home in the suitcase. Who thought of this idea anyway?

Danny was already in bed so I crawled in too. "I put a timer on the TV to make it turn off, but you can turn it off sooner if you want," he said. Danny fell asleep almost instantly, but I was too excited to sleep. I was up way past the TV going off. However, sleep did eventually find me.

The next morning my hair looked insanely crazy. It looked better after a good brushing

I put on jeans that made my butt look great, and the shirt Sam suggested. I completed the look by applying makeup. I hardly ever wore makeup, but this was a special occasion. Danny and I left our hotel room to meet Sam and Mama Renee.

We all took a cab to the Kayte Burrow studio. The taxi smelled of sweat and pine air freshener. Poor Danny, he had to sit in the passenger seat. Once the ride was over, a woman met us and smiled. She turned to Sam. "You're Sam right?" she asked.

"Yep," he answered.

"My name is Vicky," the woman said.

Vicky faced Mama Renee. While shaking her hand, she said, "You must be his mom." Vicky turned her attention to Danny and me. "Who might you be?" she asked.

Sam spoke for us. "This is my best friend Julia and her brother Danny." Vicky shook our hands.

"Let me show you guys around," Vicky said. "I'm Kayte Burrow's assistant, by the way," she added. We followed her without question. We had been told that we would have a guide. I had brought Topaz with me, and no one said anything. I couldn't just leave her in the hotel room back at the Hanson.

Vicky led us on stage where Kayte Burrow was sitting. She got up and came over to us. "Hello Sam!" Kayte Burrow said with a ton of excitement. She shook his hand.

"You must be Renee Drayko," Kayte Burrow said to Sam's mom.

She also introduced herself to Danny and me. "When the show starts, I will tell some jokes, you'll come out and sing, then Max Faulkner will come out," Kayte Burrow said to Sam.

"Kay," Sam replied.

"Let's get you guys backstage," Vicky said, and we followed her.

When the show started, Kayte Burrow gave her audience laughs by telling jokes about the President, the economy, celebrities, and chickens. I didn't fully understand the last joke about chickens, but some people laughed. Now, it was Sam's turn to entertain the crowd and the viewers at home. He carried his guitar on stage with him. Sam sang his songs. I had heard all of them except for one. It was entitled Your Gray Eyes.

Here's how it goes:

Someone made you sad again.
I sure hope it wasn't me.

That would make me sad too.
Does it really matter anyway?

Your gray eyes crying and falling like rain.
Staining my shirt, but let those teardrops run.
Throat hurts, but you won't admit it.
Your head's placed on my shoulder.
It might be going numb, but I'm not going to move it.
Does it really matter anyway?

Your gray eyes crying and falling like rain.
Staining my shirt, but let those teardrops run.
Everything's okay as long as I'm with you.
It won't be long till you're happy again.
That will make me happy again.
Does it really matter anyway?

Your gray eyes crying and falling like rain.
Staining my shirt, but let those teardrops run.
Even if you don't need my help anymore
I will always be here for you.
Does it really matter anyway?

I was shocked. That song was about me. During the break, Sam told me that he had written it the day we almost kissed.

"Well, I hoped you'd like it," Sam said.

I mouthed the words, "I did."

Max Faulkner walked up to us. "Nice songs man," he said.

"Thanks," Sam replied.

Max Faulkner ran on to the stage to talk about his latest movie.

I mumbled the word "water," to Topaz. What happened next was unexpected. Topaz ran on stage and stole Max Faulkner's water glass! I chased after her and gave him his water back. "Why don't you sit down and join us?" Kayte Burrow half asked me and half commanded me. I was beyond embarrassed. However, the show was over now. We left.

We stayed the night at the Hanson Hotel. The next morning, we rode a plane back to Spellman. Seth was waiting to pick us up. Once I got back home, I crashed on my bed for a ten-minute nap before unpacking my bag. Danny was asleep on the couch when I got back downstairs.

CHAPTER 4

Visitation

D anny and I got another letter from our uncle. The letter informed us that our uncle, aunt, and only cousin, Crystal, were coming to visit. They didn't like Danny and me. Our uncle and his family wanted Pa's money. However, Danny and I had it. We were the only ones in Pa's will. This uncle wouldn't take Danny and me in when our dad died.

Pa was my father's and my uncle's grandfather, so that made him mine and Danny's great grandfather. However, Pa and his wife raised my dad and my uncle. Pa and my great grandma had only one daughter, and she had two boys, my uncle and my dad. However, we don't know who their fathers are. She was really wild and eventually ran off. Pa hasn't heard from her in years. She may not even be alive anymore, but Pa won't think like that.

My great grandma died from cancer a few months before I was born. She was a great influence on my mom's life, so I was named after her. Danny wasn't named after anyone. My mom just really liked that name. Since my dad liked it too, Danny was named Daniel.

My mom had been in and out of foster homes since the age of twelve. Her parents went to prison for drugs. She didn't have much to do with them after that. Danny and I never got to meet them, but we have seen pictures. I believe that they are out of prison now, but I'm not sure.

We heard a knock at the door. Danny opened the door and our uncle stood there with his family. They entered our house and put their bags away. "Where's the bathroom?" Crystal asked. I showed her and went back to my bedroom.

I heard the front door open and someone call out, "Julia!" It was Sam. I heard footsteps on the stairs, and Sam came into my room.

Crystal also came into my room. "Who's this?" she asked.

"Hey, I'm Sam," he said.

"Crystal," she said, sitting at my desk.

"Can I talk to you alone?" Sam asked me.

I grabbed my notebook and wrote, "Crystal just got here. Can it wait?"

"Not really, my mom's not home," he said.

"Well, that sounds naughty!" Crystal exclaimed.

"It's not," Sam informed her.

I followed Sam to his house. We went inside and sat on the couch in the living room. "Do you know I love you?" he asked.

I nodded.

"I'm guessing you love me the same?" he asked.

I nodded my head again.

"Do you want to be my girlfriend?"

This question caught me off guard. "Yes!" I choked out, but it caused me to cough. However, it didn't last long. Sam took my hand in his, and we walked back to my house.

Up in my room, Sam and I sat on my bed. "This doesn't seem weird at all," he said. I shook my head. We locked eyes and kissed. I was sure glad that Crystal wasn't there.

It seemed like only a second until we heard, "Wow! Julia someone actually loves you!" Crystal shouted. I glared at her as she sat down at my desk. Anyone else would have left, but Crystal stayed in my room. I had to go to the bathroom, so I left the room.

"Where are you going?" Sam asked me. He had to read my lips. When I returned, I stopped outside the door. I heard talking inside.

"Why are you with her?" Crystal asked.

"Cause I love her," Sam said.

"Yeah I bet you two just do stuff with each other," Crystal said.

"Huh?" he asked.

"Sex," she said without hesitation.

"No, we have been friends forever," he said.

"Oh so she won't do it?" she asked.

"No," he said.

"Oh, so you have done it."

"No!" Sam's voice seemed confused. He more than likely was.

What Crystal said next took me by surprise and irritated me. "You should be with me instead. I will do anything." Sam didn't have a chance to answer. I entered my room.

"Ho," I said to Crystal. Sam's eyes just about popped out of his head. Danny, my uncle, and my aunt came up to my bedroom.

"I should go," Sam said as he left.

"What's going on?" Danny asked.

"Just a little disagreement," Crystal said.

"Well, maybe we should leave," my aunt said.

"Yes it seems that this weekend stay was a bad idea," my uncle added. They got their stuff and left.

CHAPTER 5

My Brother

I always wondered if Danny blamed me for our mom and dad's death. My dad had blamed me for my mom's death. I remembered him saying to me, "My wife died to save you, and you're not even normal." Danny didn't ever say anything about it, but I knew he wanted to talk to me.

I was sitting on the sofa when Danny came to join me. "I need to talk to you," he said.

I grabbed my notebook on the coffee table in front of me and the pencil beside it. "I know what you said, and I'm not mad," Danny said.

I wrote to him, "I'm dating Sam."

"That doesn't have much to do with things," Danny said. I looked at him confused.

"She was making fun of me and tried to get Sam to do stuff with her," I wrote.

"You better not do anything like that with him!" Danny exclaimed. "Only if you truly love the person or not even then," he added.

"I'm not that stupid."

"I know you won't, but you're my little sister. It's just gross to think about." That was the end of our conversation.

Danny got up and went into the kitchen. He came back with two sodas. "Here you go," Danny said.

"Do you blame me for Mom and Dad's death?" I asked.

"Of course not, Mom died so I could have you. She knew I needed you more," he said. I just sat there and listened. "Dad was screwed up, should've gone to some kind of counseling, but didn't. That's purely his fault." Nothing else was said, and Danny turned on the TV.

I took a shower, put on my jammies, went to bed, and fell asleep instantly. In the morning, I leaned inside Danny's room and got him up. Breakfast was my next task. Danny came downstairs just as breakfast was ready. After eating, we finished getting ready for school and met Heather and Paige.

Sam was waiting for me at school. "How was your morning?" he asked me.

I mouthed the word, "Normal" to him.

"That's good," he said.

I nodded in agreement. We parted ways.

My day went by pretty slowly until my last hour, which was kind of interesting. My last hour was gym, and we were playing dodgeball. Danny was on my team and Luke Jones was on the other team. They were really competitive with each other. Luke hit Danny in the crotch, but I pelted him with several dodge balls.

After school, Sam was waiting for me by Danny's Chevy but left when Paige arrived. Danny and Heather came next, then Luke Jones.

"Hey, sorry man," Luke said.

"Yeah, I bet you are," Danny said. Luke stared at him. "And besides, I'm big enough to take a little hit," Danny added. We climbed into the car and left Luke standing there. "Sorry you guys had to hear that," Danny said.

"It's okay," Paige replied for the both of us. I had heard it all before.

My phone went off. It was Crystal. The text message said, "How much do you know about Luke Jones?"

I sent, "He's mean. Why?"

"Cause he asked me out and I like him." I didn't send her any more messages.

When we got back to my house, Paige and I went over to Sam's house. He was home alone, but Mama Renee showed up with snacks shortly after we got there. We sat on the couch eating and watching TV.

Crystal sent me another message. "What does he do?"

I sent her, "He makes fun of Danny and me." She didn't text back.

There was a knock at the door. Mama Renee answered it. Standing at the door was Danny and

Heather. I was surprised to see them. Danny held an envelope in his hand. He handed it to me, and I opened it. Inside was a letter from the *Kayte Burrow Show*. I just stood there and stared at the letter blankly. For the first time in my life, I was truly speechless. Danny looked at me with confusion. He tried to get me to take a notebook, but I shook my head.

The letter said:

Dear Julia,

I'm inviting you to be on my show. I would absolutely love to interview you. If you decide to come, could you please bring that amazing dog of yours with you? I would like to feature her as well. I hope to see you there.

Sincerely,
Kayte Burrow

At home, I placed the letter on the coffee table and scrambled to shower and get back to Sam's house before the *Kayte Burrow Show* came on. Sam was the star of the show, and I noticed they edited Topaz out. I was so excited about being on the show that I wasn't paying much attention to the screen.

I went back home planning to go to bed, but Danny stopped me.

"I don't think so Julia," he said. I turned around and went back to the couch. "I know what's wrong, but you're just going to have to cheer yourself up," Danny said.

I wrote to him, "I'm excited."

"You are, but you're also scared," he said. "You're scared that people will judge you," he added. Danny was right; I just hadn't realized it yet. He got us sodas and sat back down beside me. "You know you don't have to do this if you don't want to," Danny said.

I wrote, "I know."

I texted Sam and asked his opinion. He wasn't much help. Sam just told me to do whatever I wanted to do. That was good advice if I knew what I wanted to do. I wasn't mad at him. He was only trying to help.

I woke up in the middle of the night. Danny must have heard me. He opened my door and poked his head in.

"Everything will be okay," he said.

I nodded my head at him.

"Now go back to bed," he added. I did so. However, sleep was hard to find.

I hated making decisions. Danny usually made the important decisions for me. At restaurants, he ordered for me. I wished he'd make this one for me. I didn't enjoy difficult settings. I sent Crystal and Paige text messages. They both told me to go on the show. I was scared though.

In the morning, I made my decision. I would go on the *Kayte Burrow Show* and let her interview me. I couldn't focus at school, and I considered backing out. However, I told myself that I didn't have to do the show and that I actually wanted to do it.

I found out that our school was having a dance the next night. It was high school only. Crystal was going to come with Luke. She was going to stay with us since she lived a little too far away. The dance was supposed to last until midnight. We would have to see what actually goes on.

Heather took me shopping for a dress. It was black at the top with a yellow band under the bust. The bottom of the dress was black and white striped. I would probably wear red flats with it.

After school, Heather and Paige didn't ride home with us. Heather had a car, but they didn't meet us at our house. Danny must have read my mind, for he said, "We're not fighting, but I think something's bothering her."

All the Drayko boys came through our front door. "We're hungry and we can't cook," Sam said.

"Yeah, our mom's got to work late," Shane added.

I made grilled chicken with macaroni and cheese. We had cookies for dessert.

After eating, Sam asked, "Do you have a dress for the dance?"

I nodded.

"Can I see it?"

I nodded my head again.

Sam followed me upstairs. I heard the door open and close. Shane and Seth must have left. My dress hung on the back of my door. I showed it to Sam.

"That's going to look great on you!" he exclaimed.

Sam and I didn't get to spend any more time together. Danny asked how to use the dryer. I had showed him a hundred times, but it never stuck with him. He had forgotten to get the wrinkles out of his shirt for the dance. That's what he needed the dryer for.

After school the next day, I got ready for the dance. Sam rode with me in the back of Danny's car, and Heather sat up front in the passenger seat. I would have to sit in the middle on the way home.

The dance was actually fun. Sam and I danced to every song. Some were fast and some were slow. I didn't see Crystal until she met us by the lockers after the dance was over. She was all over Luke but stopped once she saw us.

Danny took Heather home first. Crystal sat up front once Heather got out of the car. Sam went back to his house when we got home. However, we made sure to sneak a kiss when no one was looking.

CHAPTER 6

Crystal

I made Crystal a make-shift bed on the floor out of blankets. Once we both laid down, Crystal said, "I need to talk to someone."

I looked at her.

"I got a question…," her voice trailed off. "I really like Luke, but I think he wants more from me."

I wrote to her, "Sex?"

She read it and said, "Yeah."

"Has he asked?" I questioned her.

"Sorta, he said he wanted to go further with me than what we have been," Crystal informed me. "Has Sam ever done that?"

I shook my head.

Crystal rolled over so she wasn't facing me anymore. I let sleep overtake me. When we woke up in the morning, Crystal said, "I'm still debating the Luke thing. I just like him so much," she added.

I grabbed a piece of paper. "Do you love him?" I asked.

"I think so," Crystal said a little unsure of herself.

"Danny told me that you have to know, not just think," I wrote.

Crystal left shortly after we all ate breakfast of the scrambled eggs Danny made. That's all he really knew how to make except toast. Bacon was a different story.

School went on a break, and I was going to be on the *Kayte Burrow Show* in a few days. Danny and I were going to leave tomorrow. I was going to take Topaz in a carrying cage. This would be the best thing for her. I didn't want her trapped in my bag again.

It was getting late, but Danny called me downstairs.

"I heard what Crystal was saying to you the other night," he said.

I sat down on the couch and grabbed a notebook. "We have discussed this already," I wrote.

"If I catch you doing anything like that, I will hurt the both of you!" Danny exclaimed. "Let's just go to bed," he added.

I couldn't stop thinking about it and just stared at my bedroom ceiling in the dark. Danny was really pushing me to stay pure. I wasn't going to do anything wrong. He was probably just looking out for me. Still I felt guilty, and I didn't know why. I had no reason.

The next day, Mama Renee drove Danny and me to the airport. Once we landed, we took a cab to our hotel. Danny and I were staying at the Hanson Hotel again. This time around, Danny and I didn't have to share a bed. We found our room and I let Topaz out of her cage. She tried to jump on the bed, but I wouldn't let her.

The bed felt so good. I fell asleep earlier than expected. With an early bedtime comes an early wake-up time. Danny was still asleep when I got up. That was expected. I let him sleep a few minutes as I got dressed. We shoved donuts in our mouths as we headed to the lobby. A cab waited for us outside.

Vicky was waiting for Danny and me outside the studio.

"Hello Julia and Danny!"

We walked through some hallways as Vicky told us what was going to happen during the show. I kept my notebook and a pencil in hand.

Vicky sent Danny and me out on the stage. Once we sat down, Kayte Burrow started her interview process. She introduced us with ease. "Oh goody, you brought the dog!" Kayte Burrow exclaimed.

"Her name's Topaz," Danny said. She explained my life to her audience.

"What do you think about people's reactions?" she asked.

"It bothers me. I don't want them to think the wrong thing." I wrote and Danny read it.

"Do you still like Max Faulkner?" she asked.

"Yep," Danny said for me.

"Well, that's great," Kayte Burrow said.

Danny moved down a chair and so did I. We turned our attention to where she was looking. This was somewhere off stage.

Max Faulkner came onstage and sat beside me. "I was inspired by your story, and I just had to meet you," he said.

I was stunned.

"I got a question for you?" he said to me.

I nodded.

"How do you carry on with your daily life?" he asked.

I wrote, "I just do. As you can see, Danny helps me a lot and so do my friends." Danny read it for me.

Kayte Burrow cut to commercial. We were all ushered off stage.

"Thank you," Max Faulkner said to me. He shook my hand and gave me a hug.

Danny and I had to catch a plane. We got our stuff from the hotel and headed to the airport. Mama Renee picked us up once we had landed and dropped us off at home.

Danny and I hadn't been home long when the phone rang. The hospital where Pa was staying called. They told us that Pa was well enough to come home, would be released in a few days. And wanted to give Danny and me time to prepare the house.

Danny cleaned Pa's room while I tackled the dishes. Sam came over.

"Hey, guess what," Danny said.

"What?" Sam asked.

"Pa's coming home!" Danny exclaimed.

"Awesome!" Sam said with tons of excitement.

I made Sam dry the dishes and put them away. Next, we moved to the living room. It wasn't very dirty.

"Did you like being on TV?" Sam asked.

I nodded my head.

"Did anything exciting happen?"

I got a piece of paper and wrote, "Yeah, Max Faulkner sat by me and gave me a hug." Sam didn't look all that happy. He left me to finish cleaning the living room by myself.

CHAPTER 7

Pa

The *Kayte Burrow Show* I was on aired the night Pa came home. Danny said we would have a party after we picked up Pa. A nurse was waiting with Pa when we got to the hospital, and Pa laughed all the way home. He always called me JJ, short for Julia Jane, or maybe he just wanted to be reminded of his wife, JJ was her nickname.

Danny told Pa about the party that night. Just then, Sam sent me a text message asking,

"Can Shane bring his girlfriend?"

I sent back, "Sure."

"Ok, her name's Brianna," he informed me. We didn't text anymore after that. He didn't have to ask. Extras were always welcome as long as they were accompanied by someone I knew.

My uncle and his family were already at the house when we pulled up. Luke was with them. This was odd. They were usually late for things, especially if Danny and I were hosting the event. The other guests started to arrive, but Heather and Paige were the last ones and they brought their parents. This was also odd. The Draykos were there too.

Sam and I were sat on the floor by each other to make room for the other guests who could sit on the furniture. He was really tense like something was wrong, but I didn't know what and didn't have my paper and pencil to ask.

The *Kayte Burrow Show* started. Everyone's eyes were glued to the screen. Heather turned to me and said, "Bet it was nice to sit by Max Faulkner."

I nodded my head and gave her the biggest smile ever. Sam tensed up even more than before. I gave him a confused look. In return, he gave me a weak smile. Something was wrong, and it had to do with Max Faulkner.

The show ended and people started to leave.

I wrote to Sam, "We need to talk."

As Mama Renee left, Sam said to her, "I will be home in a little bit."

She nodded without protest and left. After everyone had left, Sam and I went up to my room so we could talk in private. Danny and Pa didn't need to hear.

"What's wrong?" I asked.

"Nothing," Sam said.

"That's a lie."

He looked at me and said, "I can just tell that you really like that Max Faulkner guy."

"I will never see him again."

Sam stared at me with sad eyes. I placed my hand under his chin and gave him a big kiss. Sam's hands moved to my hair. I could see what these kisses were turning into, so I pulled away from him.

We went downstairs, and I walked Sam to the door. He left me standing in my doorway. I waited until he was safely inside his house before shutting my door. Before Sam went inside, he turned around and I blew him a kiss. He caught it and placed it on directly on his lips. Both doors were shut and that was the end to our disagreement.

I was so glad that Sam wasn't mad at me. I did like Max Faulkner, but I loved Sam. Or at least I thought I did. I sure wasn't going to risk losing him over some celebrity that I would never see again. Sam was worth much more to me than that. He was not only by best friend, but my boyfriend.

Since Pa was home now, Danny had to sleep on the couch. We would have shared a room, but the couch would serve as his bed until we could get another one to put in my room. I felt sorry for Danny. I told him we could take turns sleeping on the couch, but he didn't listen. There wasn't much else I could do.

Pa was sort of an old fashion man. However, he was into some modern things as well. At ninety years old, he still loves to dress up, especially for church. He wasn't too keen that there was a dog in the house, but he lived with it.

Sam found out that Shane's girlfriend, Brianna, had a son named Kayden by someone she had dated in high school, but broke up when Brianna got pregnant. Kayden was two and half years old, and although his father knew about him, he never tried to see his son. Brianna was going to bring Kayden over to Sam's house that night for everyone to meet him. Sam had mixed feelings.

Mama Renee came to my house and told Sam, "Hurry up, they're on their way." Sam got up and kissed me on the cheek then left. I wanted to see the little boy, but I knew my place. If they wanted me to be there, they would have said so or invited me over to their house. I did feel a little left out, but this was a family moment for the Drayko's. I wasn't a part of that family, but sometimes I felt like I might be.

About an hour later, the phone rang. It was Sam.

"Julia, come over and see Kayden."

He must have known it was me since I didn't say hello. I hung up the phone and hesitated. I took in a few deep breaths. I didn't want to look stupid or nervous. Once I gathered myself, I opened the door and crossed the street to Sam's house, but not before shutting the door behind me. However, I felt like I forgot something. I couldn't quite put my finger on what it was.

I had met Brianna at the party the night I was on television, but Kayden wasn't there. He was walking around and looking at all the different people. He wouldn't let anyone hold him. He did talk some, but no one could understand him except his mother.

Danny knocked on the door. I had forgotten to tell him where I was going. As a punishment for my mistake, he made me come home with him. I was sad, but I knew I had to leave with Danny. I would receive an actual punishment if I stayed at the Drayko house. However, being grounded for a week wouldn't be that bad. I wouldn't get to see Sam though.

Just as I sat on the couch at my own house, Crystal sent me a text message. It said, "I'm going to tell Luke I love him."

I replied, "That's sweet." I didn't know what else to say and I didn't want to upset her. She sent me a silly smiley face that made me laugh. Instead of texting her back, I set my phone on the coffee table.

Danny lectured me about how I was supposed to tell him where I was going. He went on and on and soon my mind began to wander. I never really listen to his lectures anyway, but I hoped I was pretending well enough so he wouldn't realize I wasn't tuned in. I knew Danny was only trying to look out for me, and I appreciated that.

The thought came to me that Danny had never told Heather he loved her. I don't know if he did love her, but he had to a little. So I asked him. I wrote, "Do you love Heather?" I showed Danny the paper.

"That's way off topic, Julia!" he exclaimed. I blinked at him. Danny sighed and answered my question. "Yeah, I guess I do love her."

"Have you ever told her?"

Danny thought for a moment and said, "No, I guess I haven't."

He rambled on about something, but I zoned out again. I suddenly was brought out of my thoughts when Danny said, "Dang it, Julia! Make me feel bad." I would have been upset if I hadn't seen the smile stretched across Danny's face. "Julia why did you ask such an off-the-wall question like that?" he asked. I just shrugged. I really didn't know the answer myself. My mind just likes to wander.

I guess Danny took what I said to heart because sent Heather a text message. I quickly wrote down, "You can't tell a girl you love her through a text message!"

Danny read what I wrote and said, "I know. That's why I texted her and told her we were coming over." I didn't want to go with him, but Danny threw me my jacket.

Planning was not something Danny did. He was a very spontaneous person. That was one way that we were very different. I hated doing things spur of the moment. That's why I didn't want to go with him, but he didn't give me much of a choice.

On the way to Heather's house, Danny rambled to himself and said things like, "Heather, I love you," and "I just wanted to tell you that I love you." I wanted to laugh at him, but that would be mean. He seemed nervous, which was unusual for Danny.

Danny knocked on the door at Heather's house. Heather opened it and Danny blurted out, "I love you!" Heather leaned into him, and they kissed. When the kiss was over, we went into the house for a few minutes until Heather's parents came into the living room.

On the way home, Danny sang with the radio. I have heard him sing many times before, but not like this. Danny had joy and excitement in his voice. I looked at him like he was crazy. "What?" he asked. I just stared at him. "You don't like my delightful singing?" he added. Danny laughed before I could answer.

Crystal sent me a text message. "I have something to tell you."

"What is it?" It took her a moment to text back.

"I don't know how to tell you this. Can I come over?"

"Yeah, come on over." I didn't have a clue what Crystal was going to tell me.

Crystal had just got her driver's license and a car as a sophomore when she turned sixteen. Although her boyfriend Luke wasn't very nice, at least he seemed to try to keep the peace because Crystal was my cousin.

I wrote to Danny and told him that Crystal was coming over.

"Why?" he asked.

I shrugged. She had said she needed to tell me something, but there could be another reason for her surprise visit. Luke and Crystal had probably broken up or got into a fight.

It was getting late so Pa was already in bed and Topaz was taking a light nap. Danny and I watched TV until Crystal knocked.

"Who is it?" Danny asked by yelling.

"Crystal," the voice said quietly, but Danny didn't hear it.

"Who?" he asked.

"Crystal!" she yelled from the other side of the door.

"Oh! Come on in," Danny said. The doorknob turned slowly, and the door cracked open.

"Can we talk upstairs?" she asked me. I nodded, and she followed me to my room. We both sat down on my bed. "Promise me you won't be mad or freak out," Crystal said.

This sort of frightened me, but I nodded my head anyway.

"I don't know how to tell you this, so I'm just going to say it."

I braced myself.

"I'm pregnant," Crystal said.

I almost fell off the side of my bed.

We sat in silence for a few moments as I tried to let this unexpected news sink in. Shock overwhelmed me. My brain was trying to wrap itself around what it had heard.

"Can you come with me to tell my parents?"

I grabbed my notebook and wrote, "What about Luke?"

Crystal read my writing. "Haven't told him," she said.

"Call him," I wrote.

Crystal pulled her phone out of her pocket with much hesitation. "Luke?" she asked. I could hear him. "I got something to tell you." There was a pause from Crystal so I guess Luke was talking. "I'm pregnant." After another long pause Crystal exclaimed, "Of course, it's yours!" Luke's voice raised on the other end of the conversation, but I couldn't make out what he was saying through all of the yelling. Crystal hung up the phone and began to cry.

I started packing an overnight bag to take with me to Crystal's house. I knew I wouldn't be coming back home after we told her parents.

"You're actually coming with me?" she asked.

I nodded my head. Downstairs Danny had already fallen asleep on the couch. I woke him up.

"Can Julia come spend the night with me?" Crystal asked him.

"Okay," Danny replied. We walked out the front door.

I climbed into the passenger seat of Crystal's car. We headed towards her house. I typed on my phone, "Can I tell Danny?" I showed her.

"Yeah go ahead. He'll find out eventually anyway," she said with sorrow.

I texted Danny, "Crystal's pregnant."

All I got back was, "Oh."

The car ride was a bit awkward, but Crystal and I had finally arrived at her house. "My parents already know you're with me," she said. I grabbed my bag and followed Crystal into the house. Her parents were just sitting on the couch. The TV was on too, but it didn't seem like they paid any attention to it.

I followed Crystal to the guest room and threw my bag onto the bed. I didn't want to waste time. Then she showed me where the guest bathroom was. I had only been to her house a couple of times before.

We went back downstairs. Crystal and I sat on one couch across from another her parents sat on. "I'm pregnant," she said.

"What?" my aunt shouted.

"Is it Luke's?" my uncle asked Crystal.

"I haven't been with anyone else," she said.

"Why isn't he here with you instead of Julia?" my uncle asked.

"Have you even told him?" my aunt asked.

"I told him, but he's upset and angry with me," Crystal managed to choke out.

Crystal began to cry. Her parents turned and blankly stared at the television. They hadn't even bothered to turn it off during their conversation with Crystal. She ran upstairs, I followed. "I don't know what I'm going to do!" Crystal exclaimed. "What if I have to raise this kid all by myself?" she asked the air in the room. "I'm just going to go to bed now," Crystal said. I left the room.

I slept roughly in the guest bedroom that night. When I woke up, breakfast was cooking. After I had eaten, Crystal took me home. While we were in the car, I typed on my phone, "Text me if you need me."

Crystal saw this and said, "I will."

When I got home, Danny sat in the living room. He asked, "How was it?"

I held up my finger to tell him he had to wait. I headed upstairs and unpacked first. Then I plopped down beside Danny on the couch. A sigh escaped my lips.

"Awkward?" he asked. I nodded.

"What is she going to do?" Danny asked.

I shrugged my shoulders.

"Has she told Luke?" he asked.

I nodded my head.

A new text from Crystal came in, "My parents won't even look at me."

I sent her, "I'm sorry."

Danny saw this and said, "Maybe Crystal should talk to Brianna." He turned and looked at me. "You know since she raised Kayden by herself." This suggestion was an excellent idea. I nodded my head.

Later over at Sam's house, I blurted out Crystal's condition. I had a hard time wrapping my head around it, and they must have too because it sure was quiet.

CHAPTER 8

Conversation

I sent Crystal a text message to invite her to come over. Brianna was going to be at the Drayko household. I had already told Brianna to meet me at my house later that evening.

I got a text message back from Crystal that asked, "Why?"

I sent back, "I have someone you need to talk to!"

Crystal arrived about half an hour later. Shortly after she got to my house, Brianna crossed the street and came strolling in. I introduced them and left them to talk. As I left, I heard Brianna ask Crystal, "How far along are you?"

"A little over four months," she said. Quickly running up the stairs, I entered my room. My phone was buzzing. It was Sam asking me how it was going. I didn't reply to him because I had no idea how it was going at this point.

When Crystal and Brianna were done talking. I kept Crystal there because I wanted to ask her some questions. I grabbed a notebook and began. "How's it going?"

"Good, I guess," she replied.

"Your parents?" I asked.

Crystal laid her head on the back of the couch and said, "Now, that's a much longer story." I nodded my head for her to go on. "They just treat me like crap. I can't do anything right."

I wrote, "What about Luke?"

She sighed. "He hardly ever talks to me anymore."

Crystal looked away from me. It took her a second to say anything, but she finally did. "He's not excited. He didn't love me, and he doesn't love the baby."

I gave her a sorrowful look and wrote, "Things will change when the baby is born."

"I sure hope so," Crystal said.

"When do you find out the sex of the baby?" I asked.

"Two weeks."

"Any names yet?"

"If it's a boy, Brady Walker and if it's a girl, Zoey Grace," Crystal informed me.

I asked her one last question. "What will be the baby's last name?"

She thought for a moment. "Right now it's Smith, but it could end up being Jones." A frown showed up on her face. Crystal was sad when she left. Luke had not turned out to be the guy she thought he was.

A few weeks went by and Crystal texted me, "It's a girl!" followed by, "Zoey Grace!"

I was happy for her, and so was everyone I shared her news with.

Shane and Brianna had some news of their own. "We're engaged!" she screamed. Shane had a huge smile on his face. Kayden waddled into the room with a plastic toy in his mouth, but everyone else's mouths were wide open. Shane had never really been in any type of serious relationship before. Marriage was a huge step for him.

Mama Renee blurted out, "I'm going to be a grandma!" then she added, "You two make me feel old." I felt awkward in this situation so I left.

A couple of weeks later, there was a knock at the door. At first I thought I was hearing things because no one ever knocked on the door. I was Crystal was standing in front of me in tears carrying a large bag.

"Who's there?" Danny asked as he came out of the kitchen and holding a soda. He gave Crystal a confusing look.

"My parents kicked me out and I need a place to stay," she said.

"But we're so far from Spellman."

"I know," Crystal said.

"You're bunking with Julia," Danny said. I lead her up to my room.

I gave Crystal my bed, and I slept on the floor. We talked and wrote to each other. "How are you going to get to school in the morning?" I asked.

"I'll drive," she replied. Crystal began to talk aloud. Nothing she said was directed towards me.

When I woke up that morning, Crystal was already gone. Danny and I went to school. Something was different though. Luke Jones had the nerve to give me a dirty look. I marched up to him and stared him down.

"What?" he asked me. Luke stared at me then dug in his pocket. He pulled out a crinkled piece of paper and gave it to me.

I took out a pen and wrote, "You got my cousin pregnant, and now she has to live with me. You have some nerve giving me a dirty look!"

"Now, Julia!" Luke exclaimed. "This isn't all my fault. Crystal isn't innocent" he added. I rolled my eyes and walked away.

I know that Crystal and I had our share of problems, but we were friends now. More than friends since she was my roommate. The whole fight over Sam was behind the both of us. We didn't talk about it anymore.

Crystal stayed with us about two weeks. She and Luke decided to try living together, but that didn't work out, so Crystal went home to her parents. They still wouldn't talk to her, but the at least looked at her, so things were getting better.

One day there was a knock on the front door. "Come in?" Danny said and asked at the same time. Shane and

Brianna stood in our doorway. Shane handed Danny an envelope.

"Please sit," he said to them.

"I promise to be right back," Brianna said. They left without another word.

Danny handed me the envelope. It was a wedding invitation for next Saturday.

"Do you want to go?" Danny asked.

I only shrugged.

"Well I may not go," he said. I turned and started to go up the stairs. "But feel free to go if you want!" he shouted.

I made it up the stairs and flopped on my bed. Then my bedroom door opened. "Maybe you should try going over to Sam's house," Danny suggested. I must have looked really confused because he added, "I know you want to go and Renee will probably be sitting all by herself."

I went across the street to the Drayko house. I made sure to knock on the door because you never know what you might find behind the Drayko's front door. One time Seth wasn't expecting anyone, and I walked right in their house. He was wearing old boxers complete with holes and nothing else.

A voice from behind the door shouted, "Come on in!" The entire Drayko family, plus Brianna and Kayden, were sitting in the family living room.

"Hello Miss Julia!" Mama Renee exclaimed. I took a seat next to Sam on the couch. He turned and smiled at me.

Shane spoke up. "I think that we should invite him," he said.

"Okay," Brianna replied.

"Whatever you want honey," Mama Renee said. She seemed a little sad. I had absolutely no idea what everyone was talking about.

"I will give you your father's address," she said. Mama Renee left the room.

When Mama Renee returned, she was holding a little gray box. It held what looked to be an address box. Renee dug through the box. Finally, she found what she was looking for.

"Here you go," she said while handing Shane a small white card.

"You really don't like this, do you?" he asked, taking the card.

"I'll be fine, Sweetheart. It's you and Brianna's wedding, not mine. Invite who you want," she said with a smile.

"I haven't seen dad since…," Sam's voice trailed off.

"I know what you mean man," Seth added.

"Do you think he will even come?" Shane asked the both of them.

"He does care some because he was at your graduation, Shane," Mama Renee announced.

"Do you think he will come to my graduation?" Seth asked.

"He probably will, but don't get your hopes up."

"Maybe we should go to his house," Shane suggested. He left followed by Brianna and his brothers.

Mama Renee looked stressed out. She let out a sigh. I took out a notebook and asked, "Can I ride with you and sit by you at the wedding?" I showed her what I wrote.

"Yeah sure, I'm going to be sitting by myself anyway or my parents might sit by us," she said.

I got up and left. Mama Renee seemed like she wanted to be alone.

When I got home, Danny asked, "You going with Renee?" I nodded my head.

"Heather and Paige want to take you dress shopping." My eyes lit up. "You free this Saturday?" he asked. I nodded my head again.

On Saturday, Heather, Paige, and I went shopping, but not before Heather teased Danny about going with us. "Go with us! You can get a dress too," she said. Danny rolled his eyes at her and went back into the house. Heather backed out of the driveway, and we were off.

"So what colors were you thinking about?" Heather asked.

I wrote "blue and gold." Paige said it for me.

"That'll be so pretty!" Paige exclaimed.

"No doubt," Heather said in agreement. I just smiled. I was happy that they agreed with my choice.

We went to Spellman because they had better shops there. I narrowed my dress choices down. I picked one,

Paige picked one, and Heather picked one. However, I ended up choosing the dress that I had originally chosen. It was black with gray swirls on it. It had a blue stripe under the bust. I also bought silver shoes and blue earrings. We bought the dress and headed home.

The morning of the wedding I ran around getting ready when I heard Danny shout, "Julia get down here. Sam's here!" Sam looked handsome in his suit. We had to sit in the back because Seth had shotgun.

Once we got to the beautiful church, I sat on the first bench. One of Sam's friends walked Mama Renee down the aisle to her seat beside me. The wedding started. Kayden carried in the rings. A little girl I hadn't seen before was the flower girl. Brianna's father walked her down the aisle, her dress was big and covered with lace.

The reception was filled with really good food, cake, and dancing. After a while, Sam came over and grabbed my hand. It was just a little unexpected, but it felt great. We began to slow dance. My mind wandered away as Sam and I twirled around the floor. However, my thoughts were interrupted by Sam saying, "Let's sit back down." I let him lead me back to my seat. He kissed me on the cheek right before we sat down.

Shane and Brianna drove off in his car. They were going to Vegas for the honeymoon. Although Shane had visited Vegas after he graduated high school, Brianna had never been there. Kayden was going to stay with Brianna's parents, but he didn't want to let go of his mother.

Renee drove Seth, Sam, and me home. Crystal sent me a text message, "Getting close!"

I sent back, "I'm excited!" I really was excited for Crystal, but I also worried about her. I knew that she had a long road in front of her. I admired her choice to keep the baby.

"Are you excited to have a new cousin?" Sam asked as we got out of the car. I nodded.

We heard Mama Renee screamed, "Holy Crap!" We saw a man standing on the Drayko's front porch.

"Dad?" Sam asked with a ton of confusion.

"Why is he here?" Seth asked with an attitude.

"I'm going to find out. Go to Julia's." Mama Renee said. So Sam and Seth followed me to my house still in their suits.

"Come in and sit down," Danny said when we walked through the door. He looked surprised. Seth was hardly ever at our house. He usually just stopped by to get Sam, so I understood why Danny would be so surprised. Also, both boys were in suits. That probably added to his confusion. It would have mine if I hadn't already known why Sam and Seth were at my house.

I went upstairs to change out of my dress, but I noticed Sam was following me. As we entered my room, Sam whispered, "I want to dance." I turned on the radio as Sam shut the door. To my delight, the DJ was playing a slow song. I didn't have the radio up very loud so I could hear Danny and Seth talk.

"Um, the radio's playing a slow song and the door's shut," Seth said.

"Surely they're smarter than that," Danny replied. "We can hear you!" Sam shouted. Things fell silent after that.

The song ended and a commercial came on. We stopped dancing. I sent Sam away so I could change clothes. On his way down the stairs, Sam untucked his shirt from his pants. It didn't take me long to change into basketball shorts and a tank top. "Oh no! One of you changed clothes and the others clothes are all jacked up," Danny said.

"Think what you want," Sam said.

Seth started his own conversation with Sam. "I wonder why Dad showed up at our house?" Seth let out a sigh.

"I don't know," Sam replied. "Maybe it has something to do with the wedding," he added. Seth only shrugged.

"So your Dad is at your house right now?" Danny asked them.

"Yep," Seth answered.

"It's been years since we've seen him" Sam informed us.

Just then, Mama Renee burst through the door. "Hello everyone!" she exclaimed, shutting the door behind her.

"Is it safe to come home now?" Seth asked sarcastically.

"Yes," she replied with sharpness in her voice. Mama Renee let out her breath. "Sorry for intruding Danny."

"No problem" he replied.

As they left, Sam asked his mom, "Why was Dad here?"

She let out a sigh. "To apologize for not coming to the wedding," Mama Renee said. Sam said something else, but I couldn't make it out. The rest of the conversation was out of my hearing range. They shut the door behind them.

Pa arrived home with groceries. He also brought pizza for dinner. After eating, I asked Pa if we could visit the graves the next day after church. He agreed. We all tried to visit the graves yearly, but it was way too sad. It had been eleven years since my great-grandma died and ten for my mom. My father had been gone now for around five years.

I was falling asleep when I received a text message from Sam. It said, "My mom was really upset."

I sent him a frowning face. I didn't know what to say to him. I had never faced anything like this before. Earlier, both Seth and Sam had seemed angry and confused. I would try to talk to Sam about it at church the next day. However, Sam might not want to talk about it.

CHAPTER 9

Churches, Cemeteries & New Beginnings

The overpowering smell of bacon filled my nose on Sunday morning. I hurried downstairs to see who was cooking. To my delight, Pa was making bacon and eggs. Danny was already dressed and was polishing off his second plate of food. Pa had fixed a plate for me. I took it from him and ate then went back upstairs and got dressed.

We all piled into the car and went to church. Danny drove. Most of the people who attended church were already there. We took our usual seats. Church started and went through its normal routine. We did the same thing every Sunday, and this Sunday wasn't any different.

Church was dismissed, and the members started talking to each other. I finally found Sam through the crowd. He looked drained.

Sam tried to hide his fatigue but said, "My dad's taking my mom to court," he said. "I don't know why though. My mom won't say."

I scanned the crowd and found Mama Renee, then my focus returned to Sam. Time was short, I didn't have much time for anything else because Pa and Danny took me away. They led me outside and we jumped in the car. Danny took us to the cemetery. It was on the other side of town. The weirdest thing was that Pa had his name already on a shared tombstone with his wife. It had his birthday already on it. "I think you already know, but I want to be buried here," Pa said. He kissed his fingertips and placed them over my great-grandmother's grave.

"What do you know about our parents?" Danny asked Pa.

"Your father was quiet and reserved, but he had an awful temper. Now when your mother entered his life, there was no turning back. She had the power of making everyone happy no matter what."

I felt horrible for taking someone so kind out of this world.

Pa must have read my mind. "Did you know your mother had complications during Danny's birth as well? The doctors told her not to have any more children, but she wouldn't listen. She tried and tried to get pregnant. She was so happy when she finally did."

Tears ran down my cheeks. Danny hugged me the way only a brother can hug. He released me, and we all headed back to the car. Danny drove us back home.

When we got home, Sam was sitting on our front steps. I plopped down beside him, and Pa and Danny went inside the house. Sam glanced at me but then returned his gaze back to the grass. I grabbed his hand and led him through the house. We went out the back door and sat on the back porch.

Sam didn't say anything, and I made no attempt to talk either. Silence fell awkwardly between us. Danny came outside carrying two sodas. He gave one to me and the other to Sam. "Thanks," Sam said without looking up at Danny.

Finally Sam spoke, "Julia, I'm so sorry for acting like this." He looked up now, and I met his gaze. We sat across from one another and stared into each other's eyes. "I've come to a conclusion though…," Sam's voice trailed off.

My belly growled. I looked at Sam with embarrassment. He began to laugh and said, "Eat, I've already had lunch."

I left Sam outside and grabbed a quick sandwich, then joined him again, and waited for him to speak. "I don't think my dad wants to pay child support anymore," he said. I was listening, but I didn't fully understand what Sam was thinking. I didn't know that much about things dealing with divorces. "That's the only thing I could come up with," Sam said. I nodded. "My mom still won't talk about it." A sigh escaped his lips. "Thanks for letting me unload," Sam said. He got up to leave and I walked him to the front door.

"What's up with him?" Danny asked. I shrugged my shoulders. I knew that Sam needed my help, but didn't have a clue how to help him. Because Sam didn't know the whole story, there was nothing either of us could do. I turned my attention to the television.

I heard the door open. Heather and Paige entered my house.

"I thought I was supposed to pick you up for our date?" Danny asked Heather.

"You were, but Paige wanted to hang out here," She replied.

"Let's go!" Danny exclaimed. He escorted Heather to the car.

Paige began to talk to me, but I wasn't really paying attention. My mind just kept wandering. I was worried about Sam. I hoped he would be back to my house again.

Paige shouted, "Julia!" I looked at her after jumping a little bit. "Were you even listening to me?" she asked.

I shook my head. There was no need to lie.

"I was talking about how silly Topaz was acting," she informed me. My dog was on her back barking at Paige and me.

Time passed quickly and Danny returned from his date with Heather. I must have been deeply lost in thought once again. Heather took Paige home with her. I started dinner, and Sam texted me.

The message said, "I got to talk to you."

I sent him, "Come over." Sam arrived at my house soon afterward.

"Julia?" Sam asked. I turned around to face him. "When I got back home, my mom and Seth were talking about court," he said. I continued looking at him. "My dad wants custody of me," he informed me. I was a little confused. "It's really my decision though because I'm past thirteen. I have no idea what to do!" Sam helped me with dinner. The conversation ended and when dinner was cooked, Sam left.

The next day at school, Sam looked tired. "Hey Julia," he said to me. I smiled at him. "I have explored all my options, and I have decided to stay living with my mom," he said.

I wasn't totally surprised, but a part of me was.

"I guess I just really like living across from you," Sam said while grinning. The bags under his eyes didn't look as bad when he smiled. "You know I wouldn't get to see you if I went to live with my dad. That would suck!"

I took Sam's hand in mine as we walked to class. A girl came up and started hitting on Sam. I stared her down.

"Hey Sam!" she exclaimed.

"Oh hi," Sam replied as he took the paper she was passing back.

"So what have you been up to?" she asked.

"Just hanging out with my girlfriend," he said.

"Well if you want to explore all your options, here's my number." Sam took the note and threw it in the trash.

"That wasn't very nice!" the girl shouted. Sam shrugged his shoulders and sat down in his seat.

I knew that Sam could do a lot better than me, but he had picked me. Sam was the best and only option for me. He made me feel better about myself because had chosen me out of every other girl in the world. I couldn't see what would happen in the future, but I had Sam for the time being.

The rest of the day went by really fast. Paige was picked up early from school. Danny dropped me off at home and went to Heather's house. Sam showed up and plopped down beside me. I gave him a kiss on the cheek.

"I found something else out," he said. "I have to go to court and tell the judge I want to stay living with my mom." I held his hand. "This is going to be hard," Sam said.

I grabbed a notebook and wrote, "When's the court date?"

"A few days," he informed me.

We started kissing on the couch. However, we never did anything else. Kissing was as far as I was going to go right now. I had the rest of my life for greater physical intimacy. Sam had never even brought the up topic of sex, but he knew I had already made up my mind. Sam left when his mom called him. She had dinner ready.

On the day of court, Mama Renee picked Sam up early from school. When I got home, no one was there. Danny was at Heather's house, Pa went shopping. Same came over to tell me about court. I motioned for him to sit beside me.

"Well, I ticked my dad off," Sam said with a sigh.

I wrote, "I'm sorry," on a piece of paper.

"You didn't do anything wrong!" Sam shouted.

I just looked at him. I didn't know what to say or do. Pa returned home with the milk. "I'm going to go," Sam said. I watched him go.

All my thoughts stopped when my phone went off. Crystal was texting me. "Get to Spellman Hospital 'cause the baby's coming!" the message read. I showed Pa.

"We need to get Danny," he said.

I sent him a text message saying, "Crystal's having the baby."

"On my way home," he sent back.

It didn't take Danny long to get home. We all piled into the car and found Crystal's dad in the main waiting room of the labor and delivery unit. Her mom was with her, and all we could do was wait.

Luke Jones showed up.

"Boy, you got a lot of nerve showing your face here!" My uncle shouted.

"It's my baby too," Luke reminded my uncle.

"Oh so now I'm the bad guy," my uncle replied.

Luke sat down beside Danny. "Man I know we're not really friends, but…," his voice trailed.

"Uh huh," Danny said.

"I'm just worried about Crystal and the baby," Luke announced.

"That's understandable."

"Really?" Luke asked.

"Yep," Danny replied. Luke's parents came in and Luke left Danny and sat by his parents.

All of a sudden, Crystal's mom burst through the doors. "It's a girl!" she beamed.

Luke followed my aunt back through the double doors. My uncle caught up with them.

"I'm a great-great-grandpa now," Pa commented. I hadn't thought about that.

Crystal's parents came out, and Luke's parents went in. We waited awhile longer.

When Luke's parents came out, my aunt asked us, "You want to see them?"

"Yep!" Pa exclaimed.

We found Crystal's room with ease. The door was open. Crystal was lying on the bed holding her baby. Luke was in a chair next to Crystal's bed.

"This is little Zoey Grace Jones," Crystal said. You could hear the fatigue in her voice. Pa held her first. Danny didn't want to, so I held Zoey after Pa did. Luke took Zoey from me after a few minutes. There was a knock at the door.

"We better go," Danny said. We left Crystal's hospital room.

When we got home, Sam had been there and left a vase of roses on the coffee table. I took them to my room and placed them on my desk. The roses were pink instead of red. Pink was one of my favorite colors, and roses were my favorite flower.

I went to bed without showering. It was too late for that.

The next morning, Pa was cooking breakfast, but Danny and I slept in. We had to microwave our food. Then I got dressed and went over to Sam's house.

I didn't see Mama Renee's car in the driveway, but I knocked on the door anyway. Sam opened the door and said, "Hey Julia!" We sat on the couch watched TV. "My mom went to the store and Seth's with some friends," he informed me.

I nodded my head. I took out a piece of paper and wrote, "Thanks for the roses." A smile played around the corners of Sam's mouth.

We both leaned in and kissed. We didn't stop kissing until we heard Mama Renee's car pull into the driveway. She walked in and asked, "What are you two up to?"

"Watching TV," Sam said.

"Well, wipe them guilty smiles off your faces then," she joked. I got up to leave. Sam grabbed my arm and kissed me again when his mom's back was turned.

I left the Drayko house and went back to my own house. Butterflies were fluttering around in my stomach, but I didn't quite know why. Sam didn't normally make me nervous, but today he had. However, I still love him, and we will be best friends forever.

EPILOGUE

In my short fifteen of life, I suppose I faced more adversity than most people. It could have made me bitter, but I chose to be happy and remain positive. With these challenges, I grew to understand that I was going to be okay. I wanted to share my story with others to show that they can also overcome challenges and discover true happiness as well.